Too Much Noise!

'Too Much Noise!'
An original concept by Cath Jones
© Cath Jones

Illustrated by Leesh Li

Published by MAVERICK ARTS PUBLISHING LTD
Studio 11, City Business Centre, 6 Brighton Road,
Horsham, West Sussex, RH13 5BB
© Maverick Arts Publishing Limited February 2020
+44 (0)1403 256941

ISBN 978-1-84886-657-7

www.maverickbooks.co.uk

Yellow

This book is rated as: Yellow Band (Guided Reading)
This story is mostly decodable at Letters and Sounds Phase 3.
Up to eight non-decodable story words are included.

Too Much Noise!

by Cath Jones

illustrated by Leesh Li

Deep in the dark wood, Bear was in bed.

Deep in the dark wood, Rabbit was in bed.

But Rabbit's bed shook!

Rabbit got up.

Rabbit ran to Bear, deep in the wood.

"Bear!" said Rabbit.

"Too much noise. It's your tum!"

"I need food," said Bear
with a big moan.

"I will get you food," said Rabbit.

He got nuts for Bear.

Crunch, crunch.

But Bear was not full.

So Rabbit got Bear some berries!

Burp!

But Bear was still not full!

19

Rabbit got Bear a big fish.

"Yum! Yum!
I am full!" said Bear.

"I need to go to sleep, Bear," said Rabbit.

Rabbit was snoring!

"Rabbit!" said Bear.

"Too much noise!"

Quiz

1. Where do Rabbit and Bear live?
a) Deep in the wood
b) At the beach
c) In a big house

2. What does Bear need?
a) A hug
b) Water
c) Food

3. What did Rabbit get Bear first?
a) Nuts
b) Seeds
c) Fish

4. "Yum! Yum! I am _____!" said Bear.
a) Loud
b) Full
c) Thirsty

5. What does Rabbit do at the end?
a) Go home
b) Eat all the food
c) Make too much noise

Turn over for answers

Book Bands for Guided Reading

The Institute of Education book banding system is a scale of colours that reflects the various levels of reading difficulty. The bands are assigned by taking into account the content, the language style, the layout and phonics. Word, phrase and sentence level work is also taken into consideration.

Maverick Early Readers are a bright, attractive range of books covering the pink to white bands. All of these books have been book banded for guided reading to the industry standard and edited by a leading educational consultant.

To view the whole Maverick Readers scheme, visit our website at
www.maverickearlyreaders.com

Or scan the QR code above to view our scheme instantly!

Quiz Answers: 1a, 2c, 3a, 4b, 5c